AF434224

Clint Faraday
#21
Dead Calm
(c) 2012 & 2018 by C. D. Moulton

all rights reserved: no part of this publication may be reproduced or transmitted in any form or by any means, electronic or mechanical, including photocopy, recording, or any other information retrieval system, without permission in writing from the copyright holder/publisher, except in the case of brief quotations embodied in critical articles or reviews.

This is a work of fiction. Any resemblances to persons, living or dead, or events is purely coincidental unless otherwise stated.

Clint is having a somewhat trying day. It's hot, not a hint of breeze, very unusual here anytime, but especially this time of year. It's been very windy for two days until this morning, now, at eleven o'clock, it's still and muggy. Clint has never seen this kind of day at this time of year in his six years in Panamá.

Then he gets a phone call.

Clint Faraday
#21
Dead Calm

Contents

A Call   pg.   1
Mysterious Disappearance   pg.   4
Whatever Happened to Jim Fesher?   pg.   12
Offshore Event   pg.   20
Puzzles   pg.   30
Connections   pg.   37
Hanrady Rides Again!   pg.   45
Clint Comes Home   pg.   57
Sunset   pg   64

About the author

CD Moulton has traveled extensively over much of the world both in the music business, where he was a rock guitarist, songwriter, and arranger and in an import/export business. He has been everything from a bar owner to auto salvage (junkyard) manager, longshoreman to high steel worker. He started writing books in 1983 and has published more than 120 books as of January 1, 2012. His most popular books to date are about research with orchids, though much of his science fiction and fantasy work has proven popular. He wrote the CD Grimes, PI, series and the Det. Nick Storie series, among other works.

He now resides in David, Panamá, where he writes the Clint Faraday mystery series and plays music with friends – and pursues his favorite ways to spend his time: beach bum and roaming the mountains.

He is lately active in civil rights concerns for the Indigenous people, the Indios, who he has learned to love.

CD is involved in research of natural cancer cure at this time. It has proven effective in all cases, so far. It is based on a plant that has been in use for thousands of years, is safe, available, and cheap. He has studied botany, and was cured of a serious lymphoma with use of the plant, *Ambrosia peruviana*.

Information about this cure is free on the FaceBook page, Ambrosia peruviana for cancer. CD asks only that all who try it please report on its effectiveness on that group.

Dead Calm

A Call

Clint Faraday sighed and dove into the bay off his deck. Anything to get relief from the muggy day it had turned into. Even the water seemed too warm.

He didn't have air conditioning. This was the first time in his six years here that he wished he had more than the fans.

What was going on? This was the windy season in Bocas del Toro! It was normal-windy at six, when he had his third cup of coffee for the day, but the wind simply stopped. It died to dead still by seven, and there hadn't been a hint of a breeze since. It was only ten fifty. Already, the day was miserable.

It wasn't the heat, directly. It was often in the low nineties here, but there was as often a breeze that made it rather pleasant to those who had acclimated. Until now. The lack of breeze let the humidity hang there. Your sweat wouldn't evaporate, so there was no noticeable cooling effect. He had checked the situation on his computer to find there was a high pressure circle sitting there that would make for storms to the north before it moved onshore in a few hours. Hopefully, very few.

He climbed out of the bay and stood under the shower for a few seconds. It seemed almost cold by contrast. He wouldn't allow it to cool his body too much, because that would make the return to the calm that much worse. Judi Lum, his attractive neighbor and major help in his detective business – much more active than before he retired from it in Florida to move here – was misting the orchids on her deck. She saw Clint standing there nude and wagged a finger at him, as she had done for the six years he had lived there. That reminded him, so he turned on the misters strung above his own collection and immediately felt the cool.

What the hell! They would enjoy the cooling as much or more than him, so he left them on. The mist absorbed heat, and the cooler air fell toward him from the grainy wall they were against, which caused a slight air movement. He pulled the chaise lounge closer and laid back to enjoy the cooling effect. They called this a swamp cooler in Florida. He was almost dozing when the phone rang. He sighed and answered.

"Clint? John Fesher here. I'm in Dolfin Bay, near Isla Pastore. I think I'm being chased. Followed, at least. I can't maneuver well in this wind, and I'm afraid I'll run aground. I don't know what they want or why I'm ... oh, shit! I'm going to get caught on a bar, and they're coming! Clint! I need...." There was the sound of a shot. "Unghh!" Then silence and the phone cut off.

What the hell was that about? John Fesher? He was that sort of happy-go-lucky fellow from Belize. The one with the sailboat anchored off of the marina, unless he was out fishing or something such. Clint remembered coming in from Almirante in his bay boat, yesterday afternoon. The sailboat was there, he was sure. He had excellent recall, and would have noticed if it wasn't.

This was more than a little weird. If Fesher had been out in the gulf, he wouldn't go that route, he'd go out past Bastimentos and on eastward. The bay wasn't a place a seasoned sailor would use to navigate a sailboat. Certainly not on that end. Besides which, there wasn't any wind to run one aground on a bar or coral head.

Clint called Sergio Sanchez, his friend and head of violent crimes for the Bocas policia, and told him about the call.

"Hmmm. We'll find the boat, and he won't be around. We just have to wait to see who files for insurance or something. He'll have it set up so someone will collect a bundle, then they'll run off to live happily ever after, or something."

"I don't think so. He'd figure we'd look for that. We do know one thing, though. He's across the mountains toward David, which meant he left here no later than five this morning. It would take him until nearly six to reach Chiriqui Grande. He didn't stop there, so about the time the wind died, he was already into the mountains past Mali."

"Yeah. He wouldn't call about being chased in a sailboat if he knew we had this damned dead calm!"

"I'll bring my boat around and you can go with me to find his boat and bring it in. I want to see how it's set up on that boat before anyone comes along to screw it up."

"So? Maybe he's counting on someone coming along to screw it up?"

Clint sniggered. "Yeah. That's something he wouldn't count on with no wind. Nobody's going to mess with his boat in a calm. Half the province would see them coming and going."

Clint got his boat and waved to Judi. She raised her palms and he called back, "Not sure! I'll talk later!"

He went around to pick up Sergio and Esteban, an

officer who knew the bay and boats. He would sail the boat in, after they went over it carefully for forensics, or whatever. Sergio had the kit and Clint had his cameras.

They found the boat in a little bay by Tierra Oscura. It was in a place where the water was deep enough just a few meters from the shoreline for the boat to float free. It was high tide when it went in. It couldn't have crossed the bar just out from the cove at low tide. Even though the tide was only fourteen inches here, it was critical.

High tide was at four fifty, so he would have to cross within fifteen minutes of then, either way.

Clint went to the shore and along until he found a path from an Indio's dock toward the road. He took pictures and went along the path to where it branched. One way went to a couple of houses that were just visible. The other went on to the road. He went to the road and studied it. There had been a vehicle parked behind a little copse of heliconias – if you could call it that. He took pictures of the tire tracks. Dual on the rear, so it was a truck, one ton or so.

Okay. The truck had been parked there since yesterday afternoon or in the evening. Fesher had then sailed his boat down there, staged the scene, and driven off toward David. He called just before ten, which meant he could have been as far as David. That was why he didn't know there was a calm.

"... also tells us he was alone. No accomplice."

Clint was back at the boat with Sergio and Esteban. "How does it do that?" Esteban asked.

"The truck wouldn't be parked there. It would come to the side road and pick him up, directly," Sergio answered.

"I called the marina. He didn't register any insurance policies with them, except for theft or major accident to the boat. Nothing personal."

Two Indio children came to the little dock. Clint called, "Coin dere!" They called back, "Jantoro, Clint!" and Clint went to talk with them while Sergio finished his examination of the boat. Clint came back and said the children hadn't seen or heard anything, and didn't even know the boat was there until they came, just then. They couldn't see the sail from the house. They spotted Clint coming back and came to say hello.

Clint pulled the sailboat out into the deeper bay. Esteban would use the little ten horse kicker to take it back to Isla Colón. It would take a couple of hours. He had folded the sails, and would raise them again if there was any breeze, but he didn't think there would be. Clint and Sergio headed back to Bocas.

"What do you think it's about?" Sergio asked, back at the office coffee pot. "He's obviously trying to disappear. He's willing to sacrifice that boat and what was left on it.

"Incidentally, there was a hell of a lot of stuff removed."

"He was thinking we would think the locals took the stuff. Why leave a few thousand dollars worth of stuff? He might have to convert a lot of it into cash."

"Yes. He didn't seem the type to be running from anyone. I must agree. What the hell is this about?" Clint shook his head and sighed. "Did he leave us some blood on the boat?"

"Some. It'll be his. We can check the DNA. He has a pistol permit, and they take a sample. Leave an ounce or two around to make us decide he was killed, or something." Sergio waved some vials with DNA tips inside. "It was by the rail, so we'd assume he was shot there and fell overboard. Esteban got the celular. He dove and found it right where he would if someone fell over there."

"Another thing screwed up," Clint agreed. "If he was being chased in the bay when he called, the phone wouldn't be in that cove. It wouldn't ever be found, except by accident."

"So? What do we do?"

Clint considered for a minute. "For the time being, let's believe he was killed or kidnaped or something, after being chased in the bay."

"We will believe he *may have been* killed or whatever from evidence recovered to this point."

Clint nodded and grinned. Sergio wanted this end of it covered, no matter what had actually happened out there.

He decided to go to Almirante, get his car, and try to find where Fesher was. He wanted to ask a few very pointed questions of that one!

He made his first stop at the junction of the main road and the side road to Tierra Oscura. There were always people looking for day labor jobs there at dawn or before. A woman had set up a little box where she served hot coffee, tortillas, patacones, and hojaldres. She was there at about five. A white older truck came out at about a quarter after five to five thirty. She hadn't paid it any attention, because it didn't stop for coffee or anything. It was a boxy thing, about six or eight meters long. Like those Melo chicken trucks. It had the cold door type setup in back, not two doors that opened it all the way across, or one of those things that slid up.

That only gave him about a thousand or so trucks to check out.

There was one thing that helped. His car was air conditioned, though he wouldn't need it with the windows open – in normal times. He had never used it before.

He stopped at Norteño. No one stopped there in a truck like that. Ditto at the Bombas restaurante.

Nothing else was open that early, except for a little stand just before Cañastas. Two such trucks had stopped about six thirty or so, headed toward David. Both used the baños and had coffee. One was a gringo, the other a big black. Nobody paid too much attention to the trucks. There were a lot like them.

Okay. He was right that Fesher was headed toward David. He wouldn't stay there. He would be too easy to find.

Where would he go? Who was he hiding from, and why?

It was more than obvious he wanted to disappear, for some reason. He didn't seem at all to be the type to be involved in anything crooked. From what contact Clint had with him, he seemed the type to enjoy the moment and let life move along as it would. No complications. Crooked deals always ended up with serious complications.

He had enough money to live on. Where did he get it?

Clint's nutty botanist/musician friend seemed to be with him quite often. Clint wasn't there, but heard Fesher had done some music at The Lemon Grass and at Lily's that everyone said was good.

One way to find out! Dave was in Punta Piedras, visiting with friends. He was a phone call away. Trouble was, this was in a dead zone for signal. There wouldn't be any good signal before Quijada Diablo, but that was only an hour or so away.

He put the CD of Ilumanta on. He had met the group in David when they were playing in the Parque. They were Indios from Ecuador who were playing US and UK music in Panamá. They featured what Clint had always called Pan Pipes, and were much better than most of the bands of the type playing Vegas.

He called Dave at Quijada Diablo, but got no answer. He was probably in the area, looking for rare plants.

At the checkpoint in Hornitos, he found the truck hadn't passed there (!). Where could it have left the road between? The dam?

No. It damned well would be noted if such a truck took the maintenance road – but where else was there? Would anyone try to take that kind of a truck down the steep road to La Mina?

He went back. The man at the China said that a truck like that went down the road at about ten thirty. He thought it was a regular delivery truck from Estrella Azule or Mello or something.

Clint went back and on toward David. He noted the new road down to La Mina from that side, and figured that his quarry had taken that way to get around the check point.

So? Anyone who knew anything about tracing a truck would know that!

He shook his head, thought, sniggered, and turned around to head back to La Mina. There was a road there that went to the farms below the dam in the Calderas area. Two hours of checking showed the truck hadn't gone there.

He headed back ltoward La Mina, carefully noting anyplace he might have turned off.

Just before La Mina was a narrow scraped road used by

the milk haulers. The farms set the milk in sterile containers by the road for the trucks to pick them up every morning at dawn or just after. A truck like he was after wouldn't even be noticed.

He followed the road for several kilometers, until there was a side road toward the carretera. He took it and came out onto the main road to Calderas five or six kilometers ahead.

Now. Back to Gualaca or on to Calderas? The Calderas road would lead to David and the CPA, where he could go toward Panamá City, Santiago, Las Tablas, or the other way, toward Frontera or what-have-you.

He called Dave again. No answer. What the hell. He took the road on to the T, where he could go to either Boquete or David. He didn't think Boquete was even a remote, so headed for David. Just as he got to Bugaba, his phone rang. It was Dave, who said he was fishing with Mike and had just gotten back. Fesher lived off of royalties from songs he had written, mostly country, but some pop and light rock. He was good, in person, but, like the Grateful Dead, did a lousy job of recording.

"There is one strange thing about him," Dave continued. "He got into some kind of crazy situation in France and Belgium he once started to talk about, but changed the subject. Something to do with a power play by someone that didn't work, because it wasn't planned all the way. Some way to get power that no one would know where or how to thwart it. He knew someone who tried and failed.

"Google him. There's a break in his history at that time. He was apparently in Brest, then showed up in New York seven months later. He's known enough from the music that everything he did and a lot of what he does ends up on the web. That section, nothing."

They chatted a bit, then Clint headed for David. He called Dave back and said he was going to the Quiteño place.

"Afraid not, sport. That's part of the property that was stolen by these corrupt damned excuses for corrupt damned excuses here. It'll be six months or more before I can get it back, if then. I'm writing a book about that!"

Clint knew some of his property was stolen by some halfassed scheme. Things went so slowly here it probably would take six months – or six years.

He went to the Pensión Costa Rica, then to the internet.

The Google search said just what Dave said it was. He used Yahoo! and a couple of other lesser known search engines and came up with the same thing. Too much the same thing.

That could either be because it was contrived, or because it was the facts. If it was all taken from the same blogs and newspaper reports and fan club magazines etc. it would be that much the same. It still left a doubt.

What happened those seven months? Was it unknown or edited out? That would have to be resolved, somehow. It was automatically a bunch too many loose ends.

Clint did know a few people. Manny Mathews (actually Marko Bocinni, an ex-mafia don from California who was living on Isla San Cristóbal. He still had connections all over the world. Clint had helped him to disappear here. The story was that he was living on a private island somewhere in the Mediterranean) could find if it was in any least way connected with crime or crime syndicates. He called and got a promise to check what was there against what was known elsewhere.

Something Dave had said, knowing Dave, was nagging at his attention. He sat back to think, then wondered ... "apparently" from Dave meant there was a hell of a question hanging out there that would need an answer or three. It would, if things were normal, turn out to be the real statement he made.

Logical. It was the part that wasn't on the net or any-where else he'd found. Yet.

What to check now? The web was the fastest way to find

a lot of information on which to base an opinion. There was no way at anytime Clint would place too much faith on what he learned on the web. The information was almost always there, but it was something you had to dig out a piece at a time.

He went back to the fan site and checked the scheduled stops Fesher had made. That wouldn't tell him much – in itself!

He checked who had supposedly appeared with him, to find there were a lot of lesser known to unknown bands that shared the spotlight. Cross-checking with the fan sites showed that he had apparently written big songs for all of them. He appeared because of those songs. Sort of, "And tonight we have a special treat for you! The man who wrote our biggest hit, James Fesher, is here to do it in person! Get your hands together for Jim! Here's *Love in the Subway* done by the writer!"

Love in the Subway?

He found the song done live by the band listed. No Weiner Schnitzel.

No Weiner Schnitzel? Cripes!

The song wasn't bad, for that type of thing. Sort of old punk rock. It sounded like the things those Boy Bands did in the eighties and nineties. The only one of those bands Clint ever liked was The Monkeys, from much earlier. *Much* earlier!.

He studied the band's credentials. It seemed they were a garage band who had one album that didn't produce anything that sold more than a thousand copies. It lasted about three months, and was heard of no more.

He checked out the London gig. *No Room on the Park Bench* was a semi-comic number that reminded Clint of

Winchester Cathedral that came out about that time. Done by Cheezie Wow Wow. Same general type of thing, though this one was actually very good, for what it was.

Aim High and Miss was another that wasn't bad, for a song, but seemed a copy-type thing. Done by Yuppie Iceberg.

This was enough for Clint to know ... almost nothing. He called Dave.

"I never checked out anything, but those were the kind of bands that some greasy promoter threw together to do leadons for the biggies or fill bar slots. Totally produced in some office setting, tried, failed, and they moved on. You liked The Monkeys, which was one of the first that made it. It was made-for-TV and worked. They had the talent there who wrote some good stuff, unlike ten thousand others. What you told me says Jim was probably just a studio writer who had some almost-there songs. Even those could make a fortune in the market then, and definitely *would* make one today. Hell! do you listen to the crap that's popular here? One line, no music, just an electronic beat and weird noises and fat ugly no-talent performers with a bunch of semi-naked built girls shaking and hanging all over them?

"Shee! Give me a damned break! It's all crap-promotion and a dearth of phony peer-pressure. They're supposed to like that kind of shit, so they pretend they like that kind of shit and listen to the good music when no one else is around. They can blame the success of the better stuff on the old farts.

"Proof? I went into several local bars that cater to the youngest age-groups in bars. They had juke boxes. The night started with the crap, and everyone dancing, or whatever, to it. As the night went on the music changed to salsa and bachata, then to Marco Antonio Solis, Maná, Ana Gabriel, Sin Bandera, and even Vicente Fernandez – who's my age, and one hell of a talent! As they got drunker, they reverted to what they really liked. They could say they were playing the more romantic stuff to impress the girls – who were mostly gone before then.

"Okay. So these damned parasites I'm fighting are driving me crazy, and I need to bitch about something. Did I cover what you wanted?"

"I think you really did! Now I have to find out who and what and why and how – and about seven months."

"I followed that. Fesher was set up for something that he did in those seven months."

"I think it's a little different than that. It's a really long-term thing. I just don't have a clue as to what."

"Government. Military and/or police sting ... that was set up ... it won't make sense."

"We don't know enough."

"You really like understatement, don't you?"

"I have to find out what happened to Jim Fesher for those seven months, and what's happened to him now."

"Huh! He's professionally disappeared is about what's happened to him now."

"No. He's set it up to make it look like that, but that he's dead. It still doesn't make sense. It might in Los Angeles or Toronto or London, but it doesn't work here."

"He would be trying to hide from the mob ... and is on a witness protection plan that went awry, so he has to do it again."

"Doesn't work. Why would he call me?" – which answered a question for Clint he wouldn't mention to

Dave. "I still have to figure a lot of things."

Dave said, slowly, "He was on a solid witness protection plan that ... someone inside ... sold out...?"

"That's entirely possible." *But not anywhere near the truth,* Clint added in his mind. "I have some things to check out. Good luck with the parasites."

"They're as good as gone, but the effects will last a week or two more – if I can stand it. Basilio told me to come to Cusapín. He says they can stop the effects. They've done it for centuries. The crap the doctor gave me costs a fortune and doesn't do more than relieve about half of it for an hour or so."

They chatted a little more, then Clint rang off and sat back. The call from Fesher was to let him know not to believe what was set up. Dropping the celular by the boat in that cove was one thing that Clint was certain to catch.

Fesher also knew damned well there was going to be a dead calm when he made the call. He was, if nothing else, a seasoned sailor, and knew from fifty clues and from the weather reports that calm would be there.

Question: Did Fesher wait for the calm that might not have ever come, or did Fesher grab an opportunity? That part was two very different scenarios with two very different explanations.

One thing was sure. Fesher knew he was there and was closing in. That had to be part of the plan.

Whose plan? That was the stickler!

Well, onward and downward. Clint went to the Panaderia Pinzon, across the street from the pensión, for a good "local" meal, then went to the net again. He got a call from Manny just before he reached the internet.

"Clint? Your friend, Fesher, isn't messed up with

anything anywhere. He got some bit of attention by the LeMonde group in Belgium for maybe ten minutes. They wondered if they could use him the way someone else seemed to be using him for a better profit margin, but dumped the idea when he wouldn't tumble. They figured he was set up as a shill for the studio groups popular at the time. The original idea was to promote the groups with a little backing, maybe ten grand per group, try them in the clubs or as fronter, some would make a hit, and they'd make a few mil. A few, like Boy George, were promoted to the big time because they really did have the talent. The stuff that they wrote and performed themselves made it for them. The idea came from the way The Monkeys made it big for a lot of people in the business. Like everything else they get into, they overdid it to the point something else had to be found, though it's still a way to get a little richer in places like here. You see what's on TV and sells. All from crap psychological promotion.

"Nobody, and I mean nobody, knows anything about your seven months. There seemed to be a prepared story that was never used. Just hints. He was in a sanitarium. Not drugs, because he was known as a total abstainer.

"He wasn't known enough for anyone to care, so the tale was never used.

"Any help?"

"That's pretty much what seems to crop up everywhere – which tells us it's total bullshit, from the get-go." Clint replied. "Thanks, Manny. I think I'll slob around awhile here, then go back home. Either something else will come up or it won't."

"Any ideas what's behind it?"

"No. It's big. Huge."

"How do you figure?"

"Time. Mostly time when nothing happened."

There was a silence. "I think I see what you're saying, Clint. We're talking about a lot of years that were spent waiting for something specific to happen here. My question would be what is happening here?"

"Give that man the prize for the most pertinent question today!"

"Second prize, maybe. Why here? That's the question."

"Why here, and why now," Clint corrected. "Waiting for the trouble with the Indios? Waiting for the hydroelectric thing to get this far along? Waiting for that copper mine? Something else?"

"Clint, maybe it's something now, but not here? Is somewhere else...?"

"We have enough questions, now. We need an answer or two."

"Or twenty. Baby's having a fit. Got to go."

Clint rang off and looked thoughtful. He went into the internet to start checking what was happening in the rest of the world, particularly South America. There had to be something, but he was traveling blind on this one, so far.

Why would Fesher think he knew enough that he could take this thing anywhere?

He had to find a clue. He went over every time he'd met Fesher in his mind. There simply was no hint.

With the time and care spent setting this up, why did Fesher take all that stuff off the boat? What had been in it that had to be hidden?

Clint had been on the boat one time. Nothing had stuck out as being more than the ordinary. It was a nice enough boat, comfortable, just short of luxurious. There was a small bar ... that Fesher had made a joke about. A fancy bar in the boat of a person who only drank a beer or two a week! Maybe what was taken out of the boat wasn't important! Maybe what was left in it was!

Clint drove back to Bocas. Fesher probably planned for him to keep trying to find him, but this was the chance to learn what was behind this thing. He got his boat in Almirante and went to Isla Colón, where he called in at the police station. Sergio said there was a sort of will they got in the mail from Fesher's lawyer, some abogado in Panamá City, that left the boat and all possessions to the MCJBocas Corp.

The corporation was set up with Manny, Clint, and Judi as a way to build schools, clinics, and whatever else was needed for the Indigenos. That meant Clint, as president and CEO, owned the boat.

Except for the tiny fact Fesher wasn't dead.

This was meant to tell Clint to see that he was declared dead.

Was that a good idea? Fesher wasn't into anything illegal in any way that Clint could discover, and wouldn't do this if he was, because Clint would learn about it. Clint told Sergio what he was thinking.

"We don't have to worry about that," Sergio replied. "You will note that the lawyer had him declared dead by the evidence. The way the will was worded was that you got the boat when and if he was declared dead or when there was the strongest likelihood he was dead. We know different, but I won't say anything. I'll be able to keep my part open because it would be declared murder by the natural processes."

"Fair enough! I think a lot of answers are somewhere on that boat, so I'll move it to my place ... to Judi's. It's not deep enough at my deck, and it is at Judi's."

"I had Esteban take it there as soon as I got the official message. I called her, and she said to bring it there. She can watch it with it sitting at her deck. It'll be there in about half an hour or so. He's using the motor. He doesn't want to set the sails for just that."

"Fair enough," Clint said. They chatted about a lot of things for another half hour or so, then Clint went home. When he was pulling into his deck he saw the sailboat at Judi's. She was sitting on her deck with Esteban, having a tall chicha. He waved, took care of everything at the house, then went to Judi's. Esteban was gone. She hadn't been aboard the boat, except to help tie it down. There were still a couple of glasses of the chicha in the pitcher, so he sat to tell her what he knew, so far. She had talked with Manny, so knew part of it.

She finally said, "Clint? You're sitting here, chatting about nothing and wasting time. That boat's here, and you can't tell me you're not dying to get aboard, for some reason. I haven't spotted it. Why?"

"There's a cayuca sitting right down there on the bend. Against the mangroves."

"I see. No Indio would be there, and definitely wouldn't hang around this long for any reason; ergo, it's not any Indio."

"Bingo! Shall we go inside and maybe to my place?"

"Why the hell not?"

They strolled to Clint's place and sat on his bay deck, chatting. Clint saw the sailboat move, very slightly. Someone was climbing aboard. He grinned at Judi, who asked how he knew. She hadn't seen anything.

"He came up behind the boat from here. I saw him come

from the mangroves. He kept the boat between us and him. He tied to your deck and went aboard.

"I wonder if he knows what he's looking for?"

She grinned. He got in his boat and headed as fast as he could for Judi's – which was fast. It was only 200 meters from his deck.

A man suddenly ran from the cabin of the sailboat and jumped onto Judi's deck. Clint drew in tight alongside the sailboat and jumped aboard, dropping the small anchor for his boat over the rail to race for her deck. The man had run down the far side of her deck onto the tiny beach, and was just going onto the path to the road. Clint raced through her house and out the front. Judi was coming along the road, and called that someone had just run across the road and into the mangroves on the far said. He raced across, but it would be hopeless to go into those mangroves, unless he knew which way the man went.

He could also get into more trouble than he could handle if the man had a gun. He didn't bring one.

He went back, took the paddle from the cayuca, very carefully not touching anything except the part that had been under water when it was used.

"He wearing gloves?" he asked Judi. She was very observant, and quickly said, "No."

Judi brought him the fingerprint kit she kept in her house. He printed the boat at the places he would most likely have had to touch. Everything was smudged.

"He did when he was here."

He took the paddle and checked it. Same thing.

"He ditched the gloves ... or put them in his pocket. He would damned well be noticed if he was wearing gloves on the street."

He checked the cayuca. Nothing.

"Well, we know someone's nervous about what might be on the boat. I'll see if I can find it.

"Judi, I'll leave my boat here and take the sailboat out into the bay where I can see anything coming ... no, I'll take my boat back, unless you want it here. I'll get the rifle and a few other things. I don't want to be a sitting duck out there without something."

"Leave it here. I'll be able to come out if you need me, or if I learn anything."

He went to his place in the boat, got a couple of things, then returned to tie to her deck. He put the food and supplies in the sailboat and gave Judi the keys to his boat. He checked the fuel in the sailboat, and put a five gallon can on the sailboat from his boat. He got a quart of two-cycle oil for the smaller motor and went out about 500 meters into the bay. He would be in view, and was past the regular traffic routes there. He could use the sails if he wanted to go farther. He had some experience with sailboats, and knew enough of the basics that he wouldn't have any serious problems, unless there was a storm or something. He wanted to take the time to check that boat very thoroughly, especially that bar that didn't fit with everything else.

Fesher explained the bar to people as something that was there when he bought the boat, so he left it. With the severely limited space on sailboats, he wouldn't have anything there he didn't use. There was something there. The way this mess was being handled meant it would very damned well not be anything obvious. He wouldn't have a bunch of cryptic notes or anything. Clint didn't dare to move anything, and hoped Esteban or Sergio hadn't. It didn't look like anything was touched in there, beyond the cursory first examination.

Six hours of searching, after first taking digital photos of every angle of everything, and he had nothing. He hadn't done anything at that bar except look in the drawers. There was a very old list in the drawer, a list of things to replace, apparently. Clint studied that list, but it didn't seem to have any relevance to anything.

He turned his full attention to the bar, itself. Utensils were in the drawers, except for the mixer and ice bucket and a fancy silver cigarette lighter.

The booze? He looked over the very good supply. Cherry Brandy, Harvey's Bristol Creme, Ancient Age, Nikol's Star, Grandfather's Sour Mash, a shot glass, Beefeater's, another shot glass, Kelso's Gin, another shot glass, Southern Comfort, daiqueri mix (?), two more shot glasses, Old Reserve, Teague's Scotch, Everclear (!), Nestor's Rum, Old Mariner. On the first row, That was ordinary, except for the mix. The shot glasses were partly upside down? The upside down ones were after the Grandfather's Sour Mash. Maybe a break There were two pony glasses from there to the wall.

C-H-A-N-G! Changuinola?

Then a right-side-up shot glass after the B and upside down after the K.

B-blank-K?

SD and two upside down shot glasses. O-T-E-N-O

He had noted something on the list. He took it out. Most of the items were crossed off. There were two columns. The first was almost all crossed off, the second, only two. Keylimes and Ice Bucket. He could assume, because the ice bucket was there, that those two were the latest ...

something was missing.

The first column. All crossed off except baking soda, notepad and Kirshwasser. B-N-K?

Okay. Try B-N-K for the B-blank-K. Bank. Changuinola bank, SD. Safety deposit. The OTENO would then be the number.

KEYlimes! The key was in the icebucket?

Clint checked around the ice bucket, but there was nothing. He remembered, in the deep bottom drawer, was the carton the ice bucket came in. He checked and found a key taped inside the carton – that had the old ice bucket, in perfect condition, inside.

How to decode the number? OTENO The O's were obvious. 0100?

Try that.

O2890? Try that. If it was substitution it would have to be worked out.

Which bank. He had no clue. There were a lot of banks in Changuinola. Surely he would have left a clue!

There was a second row of booze. Clint went to carefully write down the booze lined up there: Harvey's Bristol Creme. Southern Comfort. Beefeaters ... this was replacement for the first row ... or was it? If C was the next one he knew it was at HSBC, a safety deposit box, Changuinola.

Cherry Brandy. Bingo!

He was going to have to get into that safety deposit box. The will Sergio had left everything to him, and declared that Fesher was dead. If he found the box, he had access.

He picked up his little celular and started to call Sergio, then wondered about a couple of things – such as that no one had bothered to come after him, sitting there offshore.

That didn't fit.

Something else didn't fit. Fesher didn't allow smoking on his boat. That cigarette lighter was out of place on that bar.

He carefully checked the silver lighter. It lit, but seemed to be a smaller lighter pressed into a larger holder.

He worked the lighter out to find a microphone and a second little transmitter inside. That one had a separate battery that wouldn't broadcast much past the boat. Clint carefully took it out and disconnected it. He grinned and put it back together, made a few odd noises, then cried, "Bingo! I *knew* it had to be here! Thank you, Jesus!"

He then went to watch the shore. There were the usual boats going back and forth.

He grinned again and called Judi to say he found something that might be very damned important. He was going to move farther offshore to study it. It was in code.

"Can we be overheard?" she asked.

"Not from there. From here."

"Did you find something?"

"Yes, I suppose so."

"You're moving away to draw them out?"

"Yes. Just a bit more offshore for awhile, then I may have to go to Chiriqui Grande."

"Because there's nothing in Chiriqui Grande?"

"It's beginning to look that way."

"Be careful, pal! This is, as you're constantly saying, no game!"

"You're right on that little point! I'll be in touch a bit later. I'll try not to go too far for a signal, but I'm not really too much of a sailor. Not in sailboats."

"Which is something that hearing can make them try a

stupid plan?"

"Uh-huh! Catch you later!" he rang off and went to raise the sails and move about a mile offshore. There were no boats out this far in this area, because there was nothing to come for. The water was fairly deep, and he had to move a little more toward shore to find a place he could anchor. He dropped the sails, but didn't tie them. He figured he would want to raise them fast in a little while.

He fixed a good meal and found the perfect spot to watch for any approach from the shore side. He could periodically check all directions, but they would come from there.

It was just getting dark when a forty foot yacht started to come toward him from the Boca del Drago strait. He grinned and took the rifle to slip through the porthole. When they were about thirty meters away he said, "I found your little microphone deal in the lighter. You'd be smart to stop where you are."

They kept coming. They stopped about fifty feet away, and a woman yelled, "Ahoy the sailboat! Are you alright?"

He went to the cabin door and called that he was fine.

"We're on the way to the canal and saw you sitting out here. We wondered if there was trouble. It wasn't out of the way, so we thought we'd check."

"It was thoughtful of you. I do appreciate the concern, but I'm just getting away for the night before I have to get back into the routine."

"Well, have a great stay! This is a really great country!"

"I definitely agree with you there!"

"Caio!"

"Caio!"

The boat started away, passing out toward the open Caribbean. Clint saw the smaller bay boat that was coming not far behind, and got prepared. He said, "It was you I meant!" to the microphone.

The boat stopped. "Mr. Faraday! We have to talk!" the man in the boat yelled.

"Before you pulled this crap, we might have," Clint said.

"You don't know what this show is about! You don't know what Fesher was into!"

"He wasn't into anything I know about. Was it something he knows about you that made you kill him?" He decided to not let the fact Fesher was alive out. He wanted to know if this one knew that fact.

"I swear! We had nothing to do with that! I swear it! We wanted him alive and able to ... okay. Be used to locate some people and things. The last thing we wanted was for him to get offed! I swear! We did *not* kill him! It may have been the ones we wanted him to lead us to."

"You have an accent. Where are you from?"

"Belgium. We were watching him some years past. He suddenly disappeared. The bicycle tournament people saw him in David, and one of them had known him in Brest. He mentioned that when he came back to Belgium. We came to try to find him and to find the people he is working with."

"Government?"

"No. And, partly, yes."

"What's it about? No bullshit!"

"I don't know. We aren't told too much. All I know is that it is something that's critical to the Euromarket. We are told the people he's working with can destroy the entire international monetary system."

"I said no bullshit."

"It is only what we are told. It is by the system operatives that we are sent here."

"So. International bigshit money manipulators are after him. I do begin to wonder, now."

"Mr. Faraday, if you have actually found anything, we have to know. We have to have it. We are to get it in any way possible."

"I don't have anything that you can use, here. I have a code that only tells me a location not far from the shore in a close part of Panamá. I don't know what's there."

"You haven't told anyone about it. We'd know. I'm sorry, Mr. Faraday. It's my job, not personal. What you have is all there or in your head. It must not go from this spot."

He reached to fiddle with something. Nothing happened.

"I found your transmitter and disabled it. You might not have killed Fesher, but you damned well intended to kill me.

"This is nothing personal. It's a matter of my own survival." He raised the rifle and fired. The man in the boat dived to the side, but was hit in the left shoulder. He threw the boat into gear and headed away at a tremendous speed. Clint fired twice more, but only hit the boat. He pulled the anchor and set the sails, then headed for the island, after a call to Sergio, who would have the police boats come to meet him and escort him back. He said to find that man in the boat. He was from Belgium, and had a bullet in the shoulder, so it shouldn't be too difficult.

He was coming in.

Clint could count on being followed, now. The man in the boat said "we" a number of times. It wouldn't be safe to stay at his place, and Judi could be in danger from these. He called and told her to get away, fast, and to not let anyone know where, even him.

"Oh, Clint! Hi! I'm just about to go to dinner with Earl and Ben, so it's lucky you caught me.

"Will you be coming home tonight or are you going on to Chiriqui Grande? You said you'd have to go there, earlier.

"Where in hell did I leave my ... there it is. The green one. By the bookshelf. Will you hand it to me? Thanks.

"Anyhow. I saw that Emmy bitch today. I told her just how far she could go with ... you know about that.

"Where is my black purse...? Okay. Well, got to run! Call me if anything comes up! Bye!"

There was someone there. She was pulling her [very convincing] airhead act. Emmy? He didn't know any Emmy. Emmy bitch. A woman. M. E? Initials? Spanish pronunciation would make it M. I. or M. Y. A woman. Mary ... Martha? Mathilda Young! The woman at the garden club Judi introduced him to two days ago. From ... France or Switzerland.

Okay. Mathilda Young was there. Judi was damned suspicious of why. She was going to dinner with Earl and Ben was to make her know she was expected somewhere very soon, meaning it would be a damned bad idea for her not to show up.

Clint grinned. Judi would now confuse them completely.

She could do the airhead act to perfection. He remembered a case a few months ago where an agent for the CIA asked him how anyone would include somebody like her in a business, the foundation to help the Indios, when she was such a flake. Clint said she's a *rich* flake, and that she's very good in business, though whatever gods may be would be the only ones who understood why. He wouldn't worry about Judi!

He wouldn't go home, either.

Sergio sent Esteban to get Clint's boat and bring it around. They'd keep the sailboat at the police mooring for the night.

Clint thought, then went to move the bottles around, just four of them, on the bar, and to move two shot glasses. Esteban brought his boat, and he went to Dave's place near Tierra Oscura for the night. He first went around Isla San Cristóbal so watchers would think he'd be staying with his Indio friends or Manny there. When he was on the back side of the island he went directly on to Tierra Oscura without his running lights. If there were less than four of them, they wouldn't be able to follow him. One had a bullet in the shoulder another of them would have to get to a doctor, not on Isla Colón. One would be Mathilda, and another would be there now to follow him, but couldn't be close, or he'd be spotted.

He pulled the boat into the cozy slot in the mangroves where it wouldn't be seen from the water. Orlando, a good friend, saw him take it in, and came to move his cayuca to that side of the dock, which would mean that he wouldn't have room to pass, and no one could get past to check, except in a small cayuca or canoe.

He dropped the shades and used as little light as

possible. There wouldn't be any indication anyone was there from outside. He got a good night's sleep and was up at break of dawn to head for Punta Robalo, where he would leave his boat at Alex's Place and take a bus to Almirante for his car.

He thought about that. They would certainly watch his car, and probably had a tracer or two on it. He stayed on the packed bus to Changuinola. He got off just past the bridge and took a cab to the airport. He took another cab from there to the police station and walked the six blocks to HSBC. It would be more than an hour before it opened, but he wouldn't be expected there, for that reason. He didn't think they had a clue that there was anything in a bank in Changuinola, but he wasn't taking any chances. That "It's nothing personal" remark told him that these were a bunch of professional assassins.

Could Fesher actually have something that could wreck international monetary movement?

He went into a little restaurante and had coffee and hojaldres. Just before the bank opened, he walked toward town, went into Banco Nacional de Panamá, then to Caja de Ahoras, then back to HSBC. He didn't spot a follower, but this would make them think he was looking for something if they had found him.

In the bank, he showed the manager the will and death certificate copies, and said he was there to collect the things in the safety deposit box. That meant a delay of more than forty five minutes while they authenticated everything, then he was shown the box. The manager used his key in one slot, while Clint used his in the other. The long box slid out and the manager left before he opened the top.

A bunch of crossword puzzles? In Spanish?

Well, this had to be it, but how to find out ... there was a page number on each puzzle. The manager didn't even ask him for a box number. That meant the numbers from the bar had to be important. Those were the only numbers involved.

He found page 2, then eight then nine.

Why more than twenty puzzles? The puzzle he had to figure was what the rest were about. Ten of them would cover accidental finding.

He checked the page numbers. The highest was 154.

He thought for a minute, then took out page 10 on the chance the T-E-N meant that, then flipped through them. There was a page 90. That would explain the final O.

Was that first O important?

He flipped through again. The page number was in the left bottom corner on some of them. One had the number under a dog-ear. It was the only one with that. Two others were dog-eared, but the numbers were not under the fold.

Well, that's what he had to work with. He slipped the papers into a manila envelope and left the key hanging in the empty box door and the box on the table.

He had to go somewhere to work those five crossword puzzles. If he could. They were in Spanish, which meant his conversational use of the language might not suffice.

He sighed. He would then have to discover which words were what he needed. Surely there was some clue to that! Somewhere.

He went to Punta Robalo and took his boat out. This time he went to the Isla San Cristóbal place and to Manny's home there. He talked with the family a bit, getting caught up on the latest happenings, then went to the den to take out the puzzles. He noticed that they had the solution to the day before in a box on the bottom of the page. If he was lucky, some of them would have the solutions there.

Left lower corner page numbers ... gave him the solutions to 2. 9, 10 and 90. Center bottom gave him 8. Neat!

Now. Which words? Across or down? Was there a clue to solving that puzzle?

He thought. It could be the shot glasses. Up was across and down was down. Or vice versa.

Page 2. First shot glass. First word across, rancho. Down, Rio

Page 8. Serena, no across.

Page 9. Frontera, frente

Page 10. Prado, parque

Page 90. Rosa, restaurante

So. The only up was Serena. Read: Rio Serena frente parque restaurant.

Okay. Rio Sereno, across from the parque, a restaurant.

How to find what, where, who, and why?

One thing was certain! He'd have to go to Rio Sereno! He wouldn't drive. If he took a bus ... after Chiriqui Grande. They would be watching there. He'd told Judi he was going there.

No time like the present. He had a change of clothes, two, in the boat. He would catch a bus to the river just before Chiriqui Grande, take a cab to Punta Peña, then catch the David bus at the school. Past the school. Make it at Mali.

When he passed the restaurante at the bombas in the taxi he saw Mathilda sitting at a table. He grinned. He didn't know who would be at the one near Punta Peña. There were several people sitting at tables there.

They passed a bus. Clint had the taxi go on to Cañastas. The bus came less than three minutes later and he got on.

He figured the taxi would get back to Chiriqui Grande in ten minutes. They would probably get the information that a gringo took it to Cañastas and would be waiting for the bus anywhere they could get ahead of it. He would ride to the dam ... to the Smithsonian station. They would be able to see who got on or off after that stop. They may have someone at the dam ... no. The bus didn't usually stop there, except for the passengers to buy from the vendors or something.

That gave him an idea. About three kilometers before the dam, a car came up fast from behind, then stayed behind the bus. Clint called the door boy and asked that they stop at the dam so the passengers could buy oranges and such.

The car was close behind when the bus stopped and the people from the shops ran out to sell oranges, coffee, cookies, and snacks. The car would have no believable reason not to pass and go on ahead. Clint waited until it stopped at the waterfall just ahead, and Mathilda got out to take pictures. Clint waited until the bus was starting to leave to get off and stay among the vendors. The bus passed Mathilda, and she got in the car, which started moving immediately. There were at least two.

Clint hung around for three quarters of an hour, then flagged the police truck taking the new shift to the dam. He knew some of them, and they knew he worked with the police, at times, so they gave him a ride back to David in the back with the officers going home at shift end. He sat back far enough that he wouldn't be seen from the road. The car with Mathilda passed, going fast toward the dam.

He'd made it a point to flag the police truck before it got to the dam. No one saw him get aboard. They would be told that the truck didn't stop on the way back toward David, and that Clint had definitely *not* crossed the dam to the station on the other side. They would think someone came there to get him. Give them a puzzle for a change.

Now for Rio Sereno. They would have no idea he was heading there.

Of course, he didn't know what he would do when he got there.

Clint got off the Volcan bus and went to the little restaurant, very good food, just past the super. He watched, but couldn't spot anyone who seemed at all interested in him or in any of the other arriving people. He waited until the second bus for Rio Sereno came, got aboard, and sat back to relax and enjoy the scenic ride.

Rio Sereno is about as high as you go where there's any town or puebla. Half the town is in Costa Rica. It's scenic and tranquil – and cold at night.

He got off the bus at the station and strolled around, had some coffee and hojaldres, then walked casually toward the parque. He sat on a bench there for about twenty minutes, then went to the restaurant for almuerza. He asked about the gringo, Jim. If he was around lately. They didn't know any Jim.

"Well, he's dead, I suppose. He was supposed to meet me three places, and his boat was found with a lot of blood. He was a great guy. It's sad."

"Boat?"

"In Bocas. His sailboat."

"The only one I know from Bocas with a boat is called Clint."

Clint didn't know her. This was to tell him this was the place – but for what?

"I'll have the coriente. Hay puerco?"

"Si. chuleta o asada?"

"Chuleta."

She went back into the kitchen. He waited about ten minutes and she brought a good thick chuleta (pork chop) with rice, black beans, and salad. It would be the expensive corriente. $2.00.

It was delicious. Clint was just finishing when an old Indio came to sit across from him and order a black coffee. He pointed to Clint's cup and sat back.

"You're not from around here." he stated – in Guayme.

"No. Bocas. I'm here to meet a friend to receive some things." Clint answered in the dialect.

"You speak the language well for a gringo. Very well."

"I'm Ngobe."

"Clint Faraday. I know. I would like to invite you to my home to talk about the differences between here and Bocas."

"I am honored."

They finished the coffee, and Clint paid the tab. He went with Truman, the Indio, to the upper road, and they walked into Costa Rica and about a kilometer inside, when they came to a house by a stream. Fesher was sitting on the porch.

"Hi, Jim. Hell of a beautiful spot here." He wasn't surprised, and didn't act like he was.

Fesher laughed. "I thought you'd have the intelligence to figure it. I was afraid the crossword things would be too far, but it seems you made the connection."

"The setup might have convinced Mathilda and friends that you're dead. The one I shot definitely thought you'd been, as he put it, offed, but by the people you work for."

"With. I don't work *for* anyone."

"What's with the destroying of international banking bit?"

"Not quite. Disrupt. What that bunch of greedbag egomaniacs would lose in a day isn't much, but it would show them it can be done."

"You can keep the banking net down a whole day?"

"Oh, anyone can do that with only a little knowledge of modern communications. It's happened a few times by accident. That's what scares them. They don't know if I can make it last a day or week or month."

"Can you?"

"I think I could. Too many little people would be hurt. I'm for the underdog. I always have been, and always will be."

"Then I don't see the object. I shot that one because it was him or me."

"Kill him? He was just a hired hand."

"Who said killing me was nothing personal. I shot him in the shoulder. He dived out of the way, or it would've been through the heart. If he's hired to kill he has to accept that part of the deal is that he might be the one offed."

"They all accept that. They don't believe it will happen to them. Typical ego thing."

"Rather naive and stupid."

"But a high-paying profession."

"Okay. Enough small chatter. What's it about?"

"The world bank idea."

"It's coming. It's necessary."

"It will be a good thing – if the ones setting it up now aren't involved. They're trying to make it something they control, all the way. They're then in total control of the finances of every person on Earth. We become a slave society."

"December twenty first?"

"It's possible enough that it scares the piss out of me. I

want to make it the day that bunch lose their power. That would be the day the world again advances. We have to stop the total psychological conditioning they're putting us all under."

Clint thought about it. He knew a lot of people who were deep into the conspiracy theory. Fesher noticed him thinking and said, "No. I'm not a conspiracy nut."

"There's a conspiracy," Clint replied. "It's not a thing we can do anything about. As a Ngobe, it won't affect me much."

"It will. That's the problem. You can see the psychological control being worked on them right now, unless you deaf, dumb, blind, and stupid!"

"You lost me there."

"They just *have* to own a Blackberry! They just *have* to watch violence movies, even in the cartoons for kids, all day? Oh? They just *have* to buy Viagra or Cialis, even if they don't need it? They just *have* to get a new digital camera?"

"Cripes! You're right about that, but is that actually connected to the bankers and money manipulators?"

"Who else could afford to produce all that crap? Who else gains anything by it? Who else would care if I do something that only inconveniences *them*?"

"Okay. Point taken. What have I got to do with it?"

"I think you're actually someone who cares about other people. You definitely are concerned about the Indigenos. I think you've established that I'm dead. I want that to be accepted by both sides. The people I was working with could be almost as bad as the group in there now. I want to see that neither side has much control. As you say, it's coming. The thing is to see that what comes isn't what's planned by either extreme."

"So? What can I do?"

"Expose both sides. I can use the net to force people to see what they are, if you can force the direct confrontation. It has to be more than a bunch of regular conspiracy nuts they've already neutralized against p-o-o-o-o-r innocent capitalists who are only conducting business as it has always been conducted.."

"Who would take their place? Unless you're that type psychology, yourself, you won't want any part of it. The thing that has to happen – and won't – is to change the basic type in control. If you get anyone capable in that kind of thing they turn into the same thing, after a very short time. They're money-oriented, and no matter how much they have, it's not enough. That's basic. It's why ninety percent of the elected officials here turn corrupt within a month or two of getting an office. They may have gone into it with good intentions, but it's too much *money* to pass up, if they only become a corrupt crook with it. You'd have to change the basic psychology, then they wouldn't want the job."

"And there's the point! They're psychologically turned into that by the conditioning."

"So? What's your plan?"

"They all think I'm dead, but they all also know I've got the thing that would make it work. Now their side will think this side will get it and use it as a bludgeon, while this side thinks they'll have it and use it like a bludgeon. You can make each one of them think you've got it, and can use it like a bludgeon on both of them. It'll be funny as hell – and dangerous as hell."

"This is surreal. Why do all these kinds of things come

here?"

"Strong economy, and the too easily manipulated politicians. Paradise on the cheap. The huge drug cartels just next door that these scum are using to finance the undercover stuff."

"Okay. So now you can drop all the bullshit. What's really going on?"

"You don't believe me?"

"Not for a picosecond. It's too much like that TV silliness."

"Do you have any idea what percent of the population would believe it? Would you believe the psychological conditioning that would make them accept it at face value?"

"You don't need that with me."

"As this proves. Okay. The real meat.

"Part of it's true, it's just been exaggerated to an extreme. If you accepted even a small part of that, I would find some other way to get the job done.

"I can disrupt international banking for a short time. One day, who cares? It's a glitch they can fix in no time. Two days, people get nervous. Three, and it starts hitting them in the pocketbook. Hard.

"Do you know the amounts of money moved around in a day?"

"Some billions, no doubt."

"Try some trillions. Lose the interest on a trillion dollars for three days and you are being hit very hard. Your budget won't stand it. The loss in confidence will be disastrous in no time.

"Four days, it starts hitting the little guy. I won't do it more than that. I'll start with a glitch that'll take about four hours to fix. You can then contact a few people and lay down the law. We want a say in who's in charge of the world banking system. It'll become more honestly democratic, or it will cause the closedown of the system for longer.

"They won't go for it, so the next one will be for a day. I hope more won't be needed."

"Is even this for real? How do you do it?"

"I can control the comp links. I can make all the negotiations go through a security program that will question everything and call for special authorization from the mainframe master." He held up a four gig memory stick. "I can control the money of the world with this."

"They can override."

"Not this. They can only override what comes from their own programs. They do it all the time. They can't override this. It's not in their equipment, and isn't compatible with their system of control."

"Can't they go to a secondary feed?"

"In four hours. This will leave them wondering about their hardware. I just want their attention. They won't have the knowhow to find where the changed orders came from or how they were inserted. It's not important."

"I don't get why I'm needed."

"They think you have it. They'll watch you for a chance to get it. I'll be considered as no longer pertinent, because I'm dead and gone."

"Which is now beyond my control, but how I react to it is."

"You know I'm right. You'll do what you can. It's the only way to protect the little guy from a form of slavery and stagnation you won't believe. It'll stop the world government from forming too soon.

"That's also inevitable, but will be after a long and bloody resistance. Maybe we can take some of that wind out of their sails!"

"It will be a lot easier and safer if I'm not where they can find me, hunh?"

"Let out that you can be contacted only through an e-mail or something. As soon as I put step one into play, you can disappear. I can handle my part from here. I have a direct to the satellites."

"When will you start?"

"Tomorrow at nine o'clock, sharp, local time. I'll contact the people I want to contact tonight and leave an e-mail address that you'll monitor. You should start getting messages by nine oh one." He gave Clint a manila envelope with instructions.

Clint stood and said, "Then I'd better get ready to hide. I think a good place would be Bocas and David, don't you?"

He got a long studying look. Fesher shrugged, and said, "Whatever will work."

"One thing. I'll have the knowledge to locate you if you go too far. I doubt this will work, but it's worth a try. It could slow them down. Screw up their schedule."

"It's already done that."

The slightly darker, heavier, younger studious-looking man with nut-brown hair and a neat mustache left the Hotel Iberia at eight fifteen and headed to the restaurant by the Hotel Castilla. Multi-Café 2. He would sit on the little outside area with the gringos. Several were already there, at that hour. Mathilda and two men were sitting at a table, and the regulars were sitting at another. Clint got his breakfast, omelet, patacones, coffee, orange juice, and a sausage patty.

Clint Faraday had coffee and hojaldres for breakfast, and nothing else. Mathilda looked at the heaping plate and slightly shook her head. They whispered among the trio, and she came over.

"Excuse me, but you look very much like a man I met in Bocas."

"That will be Faraday. He's a second or third cousin, I believe. A lot of people have noted the resemblance. The one time I met him in Santiago, and we were standing there side-by-side. The people who thought I'd aged awfully fast and lost weight said the difference was obvious. He's taller, and, I'm very sorry to say, in much better physical condition than am I, even though he's fifteen years older. Not sorry because he's in good condition. Sorry that I'm not. I'm too much a lazy type."

"I'm James Hanrady. Jim."

"Oh. I'm Mat ... Mattie Harrison."

"I'd guess Toronto? The accent?" Clint asked.

"I don't have an accent! All of *you* do! Just outside of Toronto. Berksfield." She laughed.

"I don't know anything about Canada. I'm from Iowa, and never went there, but we had some Canadians passing through, and I can spot certain things." Clint knew there was no Berksfield near Toronto.

"Small world! I'll let you have your breakfast in peace."

He was just finishing the food when Rick, a regular, came from across the road. He'd been in the bank, and said the damned machine had quit working while he was standing there. He went inside and they said the net was down and would be fixed in a few minutes. He'd waited a half hour, and it still wasn't fixed.

Clint bought a notebook computer of a model Fesher instructed at Echo and went back to the Iberia and to his room. The e-mail Fesher had set up had sixty one messages. He damned well had their attention!

Will discuss this later. This is to show that I don't bluff was sent to all of them as a reply. He put a timed send on them and went back to the Multi-Café. He was sitting there, talking with George and Irene, at ten eleven when the replies were sent. Mathilda was gone, but the two she was with were there.

He had some more orange juice and refused the coffee when offered. Clint Faraday was a coffee addict. Jim Hanrady only had one cup with his breakfast. He took out a bunch of papers and laid them out on the table. They were assay reports from ore finds that had the dates changed. Mathilda came back twenty minutes later and had a whispered conversation with the two, then they all three left. She had reported that the reply came while he was sitting right there in plain sight, so he wasn't working with his cousin. Faraday wasn't there. The report that he had been seen was because Hanrady looked so much like him. Faraday was reported to be in Costa Rica. Some Indio in Rio Sereno said he took him across and to the upper road.

He soon went back to the hotel and spent some time answering the six people Fesher noted were the important ones. He said all he wanted was a little honesty from the bankers with the people. If he didn't get it, he would damned well see the world bank never happened.

He got a very fast answer from only one of them: *We'll have to eliminate that possibility then. Be warned.*

He sent back that he was the least radical of their tight little group, and the very last thing they wanted was to have him out of the equation. Note that he wasn't bluffing about shutting the system down. He didn't bluff.

He went to lunch at the Mosto Bistro, to find it had moved, but Cecilio was the waiter at the new place. The food was good, more attuned to the local preferences and half the price of the Mosto Bistro. He would still go to the Bistro at the new location for the special dishes they prepared.

The afternoon was spent talking with a number of people he knew. Some were ardent conspiracy believers, and said the banks all were down for a couple of hours, worldwide, not just Panamá. They wished there was a way to shut those greedy bastards down permanently!

"You wouldn't get your pensions, and that would hurt the little man," Jim Hanrady argued. "I'd like to see them shut down long enough to cost those slimy scum a few billion, though!"

"A day would do that! This is worldwide."

"Then let's hope someone or something can shut them down for a day!"

They all agreed with that. He ran across an author who lived in the area and who he had seen in Bocas a few times. He wrote mostly SciFi stuff, but also some mysteries and technical things. Clint had talked to him a couple of times at the Iris bar. Peter's. He had seen him talking with Fesher once in Bocas. In what was then Bohmfalk's.

He said he thought he'd seen CD in Bocas? Talking to that Fesher person who was murdered on his boat?

"Fesher? Jim Fesher, I think was his name. He was murdered?"

"It seems so."

"Wild Bill?"

"No. A week or so ago. On his sailboat."

"I write some murder things. Who did it?"

"They don't have a clue. He was into something about international banking, and the cops think he stepped on the wrong toes."

"He didn't seem like the type to me. He liked science fiction. He bought several of my *Maita* series. He liked the idea of a machine that ran governments, because he agreed with me that nothing else could work with a galactic society. It would require too much power to allow an organic to hold."

That fit what Clint was beginning to believe. He chatted a bit, and CD gave him a CD (was that a pun?) with several of the *Flight of the Maita* books on it. Clint offered to pay, but he said there were three *Maita* books on it, and one from each of his murder mystery series. He gave them to people who liked the genre. If they liked them, he had more than a hundred books published, and they would buy some of them. It seemed to work! They were selling!

They soon said, "Hasta lluego!"

He wasted some time walking around awhile, then went back to change for dinner. He saw Mathilda in town, near the parque, and got an evil urge. He said she seemed to be all alone. How about having dinner with him? He knew of a great place for steaks. Clint Faraday told him about it.

"Oh? Do you communicate with him very much?"

"About once in two months, on the web. I only met him the one time, in person. That's when we found that my mother is his cousin on his father's side. As you said earlier, small world! I meet people here I would never think would be here."

"I don't have plans, but it's only for dinner and conversation. I don't play the local games to try to get money from you with promises."

"Oh! That's refreshing! The local girls look at a gringo and say, 'Money! House! Car!' and can't seem to see past that."

They went to Las Brasas. She tried to get him to talk about Clint a few times, but he said he really didn't know much, except that he was the second person to be honored with a declaration that he was Ngobe, and that he was getting quite a reputation as a good detective, or something.

He left her at the Alcalá about eleven, and went to his hotel to discover that the room had been searched, very thoroughly. The computer's hard drive was exchanged after he used it for the e-mail. That one was in his pocket.

There was probably some kind of surveillance stuff around, so he acted very normally, checked his e-mail, sent a couple, and went to bed. He was going to bore them out of their skulls if they kept watching him.

They wouldn't. Now. Mathilda was certain he didn't have any connection with Clint Faraday.

The next morning he sent the second message to the six. Fesher had sent him a coded e-mail, and suggested he send it to four others. They were in the group he was working with until he found that they were the same kind of worms.

I am aware you think you can stop me and control my actions. I also received a rather pointed threat and will give you the answer I gave that one: I am the least radical of a group. The last thing you want is for anything to happen to me.

I will give you just today to consider a little compromise. If I receive too little response I will have to prove once again that I don't bluff.

I am not interested in some silly contract that you will simply not honor. That is your proven method of doing business. I will want enough public participation that you can't hold total control. Not any faction among you.

It is eight o'clock here (that would suggest Costa Rica). You have twenty four hours to make positive reply.

He sent the messages and went to breakfast. The talk was about the treatment the Indios were getting, and how they agreed with them. This was another example of a corrupt government stealing their land. He wondered how Dave was reacting. He remembered a time before when the Indios were being exploited. If he got pissed enough they might not need this to prevent a world bank or anything else.

He spent the day being so ordinary you could puke, and went to bed early. He didn't get any responses to his e-mails.

In the morning, Clint checked the computer and changed the hard drive, then went to breakfast at Doña Amelias.

What a coincidence! Mathilda and her two friends came in with another man who had his left arm in a sling!

Mathilda got her breakfast at the buffet, as did her companions, then they came over and asked if they could join him. He said he would welcome a little company. His Spanish wasn't very good, but he couldn't eat the same thing every morning, so went to different places. He had a plate heaped with hidago (fried liver and onions), hojaldres, sphagetti, tortillas, and something he liked he didn't know the name of. And a large orange juice and a glass of water.

They chatted about David and Bocas. Clint said he'd been to Bocas twice, and sort of liked the place, but it was getting awfully touristy and expensive. It was a party town, and he wasn't the party type. Mathilda's celular rang at about the same time the other three got calls. She talked in French a moment, as did the others. Clint didn't know much French, but knew they were being informed that the banking net was down again. He almost laughed out loud when they made excuses, each a different one, to suddenly leave.

How sad! They didn't get to eat more than a third of their breakfast!

Clint leisurely finished his own breakfast and went to the parque. Everyone was complaining that the bank was down again. It was getting to be a real pain in the ass to stand in line half an hour only to be told the machines went down. This time the regular internet wasn't affected. Only the banking machines.

That was to be the really scary part for the bankers. They were used to being offline when the net was down. Now they were offline while the net was operating fine. A couple of overdressed gringos were there with their lawyers, whining that they had to get the money transferred today or they could lose the deal. From what Clint could hear, they were afraid the old woman they were dealing with would find out about her house being worth more than four times what they were paying, even on the local market. Until they had the money, she could change her mind.

Clint made it a point to get a good look at the papers one of the lawyers was waving around, claiming he would lose his big commission if this fell apart now. He saw the name of the woman, and the location of the house. He didn't have anything else to do, so went out toward Pedregal to find the place and get into a small conversation with the woman. He said he liked the house, though it did need some repairs. He offered her more than twice what she was supposed to get. She said she had already made an agreement, but it was for less. She didn't need money except for a thousand dollars, so didn't much care if she got screwed in the deal. She had inherited the place, and hadn't ever liked it. All her friends were in Dolegita, where she also had a house she wanted to move back to.

"I'll be honest. Those people are giving gringos a bad reputation because of the way they make these deals. You don't have to sell it to them if you find they weren't being honest with you. It was for others that you should tell them the offer he made and say they could meet it or forget it. They want the property, and would still be getting it for far less than it's worth. They'll meet the offer."

She grinned. "I can use the extra money to send my granddaughter to university."

He saluted, chatted a bit more, and headed back to the Iberia. He stayed in his room for about an hour, and left again. He didn't put in the new hard drive. Fesher said he shouldn't answer anything until the "crisis" was over.

He went out and back to Parque Cervantes. The atmosphere was changed. The bigshots were getting very nervous. The machines hadn't come back online before the banks closed. They couldn't even use the ATM's, and were worried about the inconvenience to them being extended for any length of time.

He went to dinner at La Tipica, then went to the Siete Mares Bar to talk with Ulyses. He wasn't recognized, even by the people he was around most in his natural look. A bunch of gringos came in, and he got busy. Clint would mix and talk, while Jim was more reclusive, so soon left.

He went to Sandy's Bar and had a good time chatting about soccer. A big game was on the TV. Panamá vs. Guatemala. It was close. Panamá won by a goal.

He went to the hotel at midnight and slept until five. He waited until seven to go to breakfast. No one was around from before, and Mathilda and company didn't show up.

He went back to the hotel and got his computer. He took it to the Iris Hotel and got a room for the day and night when he was sure no one was trailing him anymore. They had lost interest.

He couldn't believe all the e-mails he was getting. Half were threatening him with all kinds of mayhem and death, and half were whining about how much they had lost.

Those, he answered with: *DUH! That was the object* and

the rest with *Let me know when you are ready to discuss this. If you try any of your regular tricks you get another little lesson.*

Ten minutes later he started getting a second round. A few were willing to discuss "options" in private. Clint answered that it was made clear from the first that negotiations were to be semi-public on the net.

In the afternoon he had five who would go on the net for the primary with the stipulation that only general issues were to be discussed, at this time. Three from the opposing side and two from Fresher's group.

That gave Clint an idea. He contacted two of the more reasonable people he'd met who seemed genuinely to be interested in stopping the takeover by the present greedy group, and who had suggested ways to slow them down, if not stop them. He had to do that in Clint's name, but said they were suggested by him to participate if they would. Everyone would be identified by a code number. Their names wouldn't be used for the first round or two.

Fesher called him and said this was all posing and posturing. Nothing would be accomplished unless they could get more of them involved. Clint argued that it would be a good time to do a little politicking of their own. Fesher said he didn't see that it would hurt anything. The debate would start at eight. Clint got all the people he could from the conspiracy group. They were to contact everyone they could, anywhere, regardless of their views. He wanted all phases covered. This was the opportunity for everyone to be heard. He gave the website address. The whole world could participate, but it was to be understood that there were to be no tirades or rants. This was serious question and answer. Everyone would have a chance to justify his position.

It was going to be a wild party! Fesher had turned out to be a true genius in computer science, and had a site set up that would work like a chat, but up to fifty messages could be exchanged at any one time. Something reasonable and acceptable by the vast majority could be worked out. If the opposing viewpoint was intransigent, they could soon learn where the real power was. The hard way. Remember: Don't preach or rant. It was solely to his discretion who got blocked. Once blocked, you couldn't get on again.

The first dozen or so were from extreme conspiracy believers. They were almost fanatical, and insisted in bringing up most of the most avid propagandists. The next few were the extreme "conservatives" who based absolutely everything in their lives on money. Then a few more of both. He still had hundreds of messages coming at a time. He recorded them all and put the ones that seemed most reasonable on the main screen with four small boxes carrying messages along the bottom of the screen. Replies were to a numbered message box. There were more than three thousand messages in less than twenty minutes, coming from almost everywhere. That would do what Clint wanted done. There were more and more hits as people learned of the site over the world. It soon overwhelmed Clint, who let the automatic program select which messages to show in the various screens, and often answers to the number of the message. After an hour with the numbers going steadily up, he turned the computer off, changed the hard drive, and went back to the Iberia. There were seven people there with laptops who were watching, and even sending messages. It was working. Fesher hadn't figured everything.

He went up to bed. It had been a very trying day.

He hoped he had figured Fresher the way he tried.

"... countered on the internet that is still in process. The site is psychconspiracystop at freshnesser dot com slash blog. (That was shown on the bottom of the screen.) and is concerned with the idea of a world bank, pro and con. The latest consensus seems to be that there should be such a thing, but that it must be strongly controlled in a much more inclusive way than has as of yet been proposed. The number of hits is shown in the top right of the screen. It has reached more than a million and a half. One participant suggested a poll that offers six possibilities. Number one, as stated, is that there should be a single world currency and world banking control, but it must be in a much more inclusive form.

"This reporter went to the site and has voted for exactly that.

"We have not been able to determine who or from where the blogsite originates. One of those computer experts employed by this station said they were emanating from Panamá for the first two hours, then from an untraceable site, then from Costa Rica, then from Germany. It is now back to an untraceable site. Our expert says it can't be stopped, and that all points of origin are probably automatic. Only one person they have encountered could have done such a thing, but that person is dead. Whoever or wherever, I want to personally thank whoever set it up. It is a needed thing. We ... one moment." She read a paper someone handed her. She could be seen getting pissed. She cried, "I will go to another subject when there is one of more importance! *No* one can tell me what I will report on! This is outrageous!

"My friends, some bunch of stupid politicians and bankers are threatening to withdraw advertisements unless I immediately go to another story. You will know exactly who they are when the advertisements stop because I will *not* be intimidated by those people because public opinion does not find favor with them."

Suddenly the screen scrambled and a message came on that they were experiencing technical problems. Clint laughed out loud. That had to be the absolutely stupidest thing anyone could have done. The reporter came on again four minutes later with a smirk on her face. "There was a serious accident in Santiago where one life was lost when a truck carrying concrete blocks overturned and a man by the roadside was crushed.

"Now back to the subject of the moment. The participation of the public worldwide is truly amazing. We will follow...." Clint soon turned it off. He couldn't quite believe they had done that. "Technical difficulties" on the screen at that particular point was unbelievably stupid.

His celular buzzed. "I suppose you're bugged there, so don't say anything. I scrambled their broadcast for thirty seconds. It seemed to be the timely thing to do.

"You're amazing! You have the whole damned world backing you now!"

"Yes. It could get some attention. I'm watching that thing on TV about the world bank. It seems someone has found a way to get the word out. I sort of like the idea of a world bank with, as the reporter said, very wide control and participation. I think I'll go to the thing and vote for that."

"I already did. Do you see what that part about their

expert saying only one could do it who's dead says? Talk later."

It says one of those two groups has a man at that station, Clint thought. *It also says they haven't a clue as to how to stop it.*

He went back to the Hotel Iris with his comp and put the hard drive in, then monitored for a little while. There were more and more people jumping on it, but now it was all repeat endlessly, and other things were beginning to be brought in. He called Fresher and suggested the site suddenly stop. Fesher agreed, but wouldn't do it in a way that suggested the groups had done it. That could cause a climax far too early, and a really bad result.

Your attention! Please! came across the screen. *This site has covered the subject very thoroughly. The general public now is aware that many of the stories they have been hearing are true. You are now starting to bring in subjects that are not a part of this discussion. This site will now drop offline. It will go online again when there is reason and logic for doing so. Please apply all the pressure you can bring on the bankers and politicians to propose a plan with the controls suggested by you, the people, on this site. We have demonstrated that we have the power. We must use it wisely. We thank each and every one of you for you participation in this experiment.*

After one minute the screen went to a series of hundreds of thumbnails of flags. It then went offline entirely.

Now the real result would begin forming. He figured it would take a few days. If Clint had figured it right, things would get a lot quieter now, and deals would be made – with concessions by all sides. Maybe something halfway decent would come of it. He felt he had stopped the real danger – that might have been the best thing. It just concentrated the power to a much too small base.

He went back to the hotel, gathered his things, and headed for Bocas. Jim Hanrady got off the bus in Chiriqui Grande and went into the restroom at the Bombas. Clint Faraday came out a few minutes later and caught the Chiriqui Grande bus for Almirante. He was home by four thirty. He went to the police station and talked with Sergio, who asked if he could close the case.

"Call it closed, but leave it dormant, with possible further involvement or whatever you label those kinds of things," Clint suggested. "He might still be murdered, but it would then be a revenge killing."

"You've talked with him? You know what this is about?"

"The banking thing."

"That was him?"

"Not the TV part."

"That was *you!*?"

"Uh-huh. I had to do something to stop something else. It might not have been the best thing. We'll never know. It might have saved a lot of people from a form of slavery."

"We're already slaves to those people. Economic slavery."

"This would be a far more benign slavery. It would be something that would take the drive out of the people. The road to hell is paved with good intentions."

"The form of slavery will change from a bunch of groups of money controllers to a worldwide group, but this could be good. We've all said a world money system had to come, someday. You've already seen that the average schmuck won't totally lose control. It'll deteriorate through politics."

"Yes. We have some time now. We didn't last week."

Sergio thought about it, then nodded sadly.

"Judi's not around?" Clint asked. "I went by her place. The boat's still there."

"She's on Cristóbal. At Manny's."

Clint went home and called her, spoke with Manny and family, then sat back with a tall tequila and grapefruit juice with a hint of cloves. He was just getting relaxed when the celular buzzed. He answered it.

"Clint? Jim Fesher."

"Hi. How are things."

"I wasn't trying to get personal power, Clint. Honest! What gave me away?"

"CD. Books about a civilization being run by machines."

"It would work, Clint."

"Yes. That would be the problem. You didn't consider the most important point, one that CD covered in the third book."

"You've read his stuff?"

"A few. He makes it plain from the first that such a thing would only work where there are different worlds involved. One world and you have a kind of slavery that would defeat the idea of societal dynamics. Can you see that?"

There was a long silence. "I think I see what you mean. I could work it out, I'm sure."

"Work it out *before* you turn the whole world into a socialism experiment. The thing expressed time and time again is the thing that would defeat you for ignoring it. 'The best rule is the least rule.' One world, and you have a structured socialism that would be next to impossible to break. Rules would be added constantly."

"I would see they weren't. It would be to the individual city or country to enforce or ignore what the machines call for. That's also stressed in the books."

"Which would work just fine with a machine emperor, like the books. A truly intelligent machine emperor, not a programmed machine. As also often stressed in the books. A programmed machine is the alter ego of the pro-grammer."

"I could ... I'd have to ... I mean...."

"There would have to be an emperor, a dictator. It would have to be you. When you kick off, what do you have?"

"I have to consider that. I *have* considered that. I really don't have an answer."

"If you can find an answer, come back to me and, if I agree – and I'm as fallible as the next guy – we'll go for it."

"Deal! I like you, Clint Faraday!"

"I like you, too. If I didn't, this would have turned out very differently. If you were half as bad as what we've both been fighting you really *would* have ended up dead in the bay."

He laughed. "I knew that about you before I decided to try to use you. I also had some pretty convincing evidence that you can't be used. I depended on that. It worked!"

"Checks and balances."

"Which is what we have to work into the system. You may be right, that it may not be reasonably possible. I'll keep trying."

"We all will. Even them. Don't forget that! We can be part of the checks and balances on another level. We do have that little point, don't we? We've demonstrated that we can do more than protest in a system that's psychologically resistant to hearing."

"Which will keep the hounds at bay awhile. Enough cliches?"

"I think it'll do."

Clint Faraday laid back in the plastic chaise lounge on the deck of his house on Saigon Bay. Judy Lum, his very attractive oriental neighbor, handed him a tequila and grapefruit drink. Ben and Earl, two close friends and neighbors who were gay were cooking the corvina dinner. Earl was a master chef, so it would be truly spectacular. Sergio Sanchez, sort of head of homicide for the Bocas Policia Nacional, was watching the TV.

"Well, it's still going on. They're telling everyone about a few more websites that are into the banking thing. The bankers and manipulators are running scared. It seems you and that Fesher character actually changed a thing or two!"

"We can hope!" Judi exclaimed.

"Here comes Dave! Hi, Dave!" Ben cried

"You have a surprise guest," Dave announced, as he came in. "He's cleaning up at the Suites, then he'll be over. He should already be here.

"What's the main subject under discussion tonight? Fishing? Swimming? Snorkeling? Women?"

"No. Men," Earl said.

"No men. That's my problem," Judi put in.

"BS!" Earl cried. "I saw that *gorgeous* guy you were with last night!"

"I was joking," Judi said innocently.

There was a call from in front. "Buenos!"

"Come on in!" Dave yelled back. "We're on the deck."

Jim Fesher came strolling in. They all greeted him.

"Aren't you afraid some of those bigshit money people

will knock you over?" Judi asked.

"Hah! They wouldn't dare!" Dave said. "That would cause a few million people to start knocking *them* off all over the world. We've had a bellyful of them, already."

"Let's talk about something else. Money people and their schemes bore me no end," Jim said. "I see my boat is there at Judi's deck! Thanks for watching it for me. I do love that hole in the water I have to keep pouring money into."

"James Fesher, I place you under arrest for making false charges brought due to fraudulent representation that you have been assassinated. I don't have to Miranda you here." Sergio said, taking out his handcuffs.

"What the hell!?!" Jim screeched.

"Oh, yes. That's right, you know. You did cost the police department – well, Clint – a hell of a lot of money and time," Judi said reasonably.

"What the hell!?!" Jim yelled again.

This would go on all night.

C. D. Moulton's works are available on most major outlets as printed or e-books. CD writes the CD Grimes, PI mysteries, the Det. Lt. Nick Storie mysteries, the Clint Faraday mysteries, the Flight of the Maita science fiction series, books on orchid culture and many others of many types. Mystery, adventure, intrigue, science fiction, fantasy, para-normal, mild erotica, and factual.

www.ingramcontent.com/pod-product-compliance
Lightning Source LLC
Chambersburg PA
CBHW071237130726
47998CB00003B/992